Dear Parent:
Your child's love of readi

Every child learns to read in a different way and at his or her own speed. You can help your young reader improve and become more confident by encouraging his or her own interests and abilities. You can also guide your child's spiritual development by reading stories with biblical values and Bible stories, like I Can Read! books published by Zonderkidz. From books your child reads with you to the first books he or she reads alone, there are I Can Read! books for every stage of reading:

SHARED READING
Basic language, word repetition, and whimsical illustrations, ideal for sharing with your emergent reader.

BEGINNING READING
Short sentences, familiar words, and simple concepts for children eager to read on their own.

READING WITH HELP
Engaging stories, longer sentences, and language play for developing readers.

READING ALONE
Complex plots, challenging vocabulary, and high-interest topics for the independent reader.

ADVANCED READING
Short paragraphs, chapters, and exciting themes for the perfect bridge to chapter books.

I Can Read! books have introduced children to the joy of reading since 1957. Featuring award-winning authors and illustrators and a fabulous cast of beloved characters, I Can Read! books set the standard for beginning readers.

A lifetime of discovery begins with the magical words **"I Can Read!"**

Visit www.icanread.com for information on enriching your child's reading experience.
Visit www.zonderkidz.com for more Zonderkidz I Can Read! titles.

Two people are better than one. They can help
each other in everything they do.
—*Ecclesiastes 4:9*

www.zonderkidz.com

Super Ace and the Thirsty Planet
Text copyright © 2009 by Cheryl Crouch
Illustrations copyright © 2009 by Matt Vander Pol

Requests for information should be addressed to:
Zonderkidz, *Grand Rapids, Michigan 49530*

Library of Congress Cataloging-in-Publication Data

Crouch, Cheryl, 1968-
    Super Ace and the thirsty planet / story by Cheryl Crouch ; pictures by Matt Vander Pol.
        p. cm. -- (I can read! Level 2)
        ISBN 978-0-310-71699-0 (softcover)
        [1. Superheroes--Fiction. 2. Christian life--Fiction.] I. Vander Pol, Mat, 1972- ill. II. Title.
    PZ7.C8838Su 2009
    [E]--dc22   2008038657

Art Direction & Design: Jody Langley

Printed in China

09 10 11 12 • 4 3 2

ZONDERkidz I Can Read! — READING 2 WITH HELP

Super Ace and the Thirsty Planet

story by Cheryl Crouch

pictures by Matt Vander Pol

Super Ace and Sidekick Ned
flew through deep, dark space.

BEEP! BEEP! BEEP!

Super Ace said, "My super phone
is calling us to Planet Woop!"

Wooper met them on Planet Woop.

The planet looked dry and brown.

Wooper said, "Help us!"

Super Ace puffed up his chest.

"I am a superhero. How can I help?"

Wooper started to cry.

"The big river dried up," he said.

"We do not have water.

We are so thirsty!"

Sidekick Ned said, "I am sorry.

It is bad to be thirsty."

Super Ace said,

"Sidekick Ned, do not talk.

Just stand beside me.

That is what a sidekick does."

Sidekick Ned nodded.

Super Ace sniffed with his nose.

"Maybe you will feel better
if you take a bath, Wooper.
At least you will smell better."
Wooper cried harder.
"We cannot take a bath,
because we do not have water.
We do not want to stink. Yuck!"

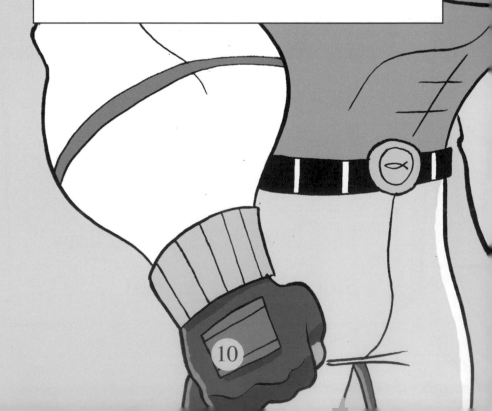

Super Ace said, "I will help."

"Thank you!" said Wooper. "How?"

Super Ace fluffed his perfect hair.

He pumped his strong arms.

"I will use both my superpowers.

I am good looking, and I am strong."

"How can good looks help?"

asked Wooper.

Super Ace smiled and said,

"Your people can look at me

while I use my strong arms.

My good looks will cheer them up."

"Water is in the ground,"
Super Ace said.
"I will dig it up for you.
Then you can get a drink
and take a bath."

Super Ace dug and dug.

SWOOSH! SWOOSH!

He made a big pile of sand.

Soon no one could see Super Ace

and his good looks.

He was too deep in the ground.

"I will find water any time now,"

he called.

Super Ace came out of the hole.

He had messy hair and a dirty face.

He said, "Sorry. No water here."

The people of Woop cried sad tears.

So did stinky, filthy Super Ace.

Wooper asked Sidekick Ned,

"Do you have a superpower?"

"Humph!" snorted Super Ace.

"Ned is only wise.

My superpowers can't help.

How can my small sidekick help?"

Ned said, "I have an idea.

I will go up the dry riverbed."

The people of Woop followed him.

Ned found a large rock.

"See?" asked Ned.

"This rock blocks the water.

The river cannot flow."

The people cheered for Ned.

"Yippee! You are a real hero."

Super Ace looked sad.

"Do not cheer yet," Ned told them.

"I found the rock, but it is huge.

I cannot move it.

Only one man can."

"Do you mean me?" asked Super Ace.

"You need my help, Sidekick Ned?"

"Yes," Ned said.

"Will you please move the rock?"

Super Ace puffed out his chest.

"I will."

He pushed the large rock.

The water rushed down the riverbed.

"Yippee!" the people shouted.

"We can drink! We can take baths!"

Super Ace smiled.

"We will all smell better,

and that is good."

Wooper shook Super Ace's hand.

He said, "Thank you, Super Ace!"

Super Ace said, "Thank both of us.

Sidekick Ned and I worked together.

And now I must help others.

I mean, we must help others."

Then Super Ace and Sidekick Ned
flew back into deep, dark space.